Teresa Bateman

Leprechaun Gold

illustrated by Rosanne Litzinger

Holiday House/New York

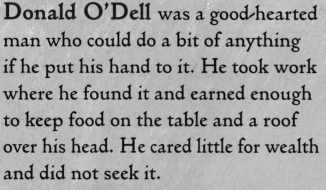

Donald O'Dell was a good-hearted man who could do a bit of anything if he put his hand to it. He took work where he found it and earned enough to keep food on the table and a roof over his head. He cared little for wealth and did not seek it.

True, he lacked a wife and family. This caused him some sorrow, but there was time enough for starting a family in the future. Still, when he saw a wife give her husband a loving smile or a child grasp a father's hand, his heart felt an emptiness that the work could not fill.

One day, as Donald was walking
through a high meadow on his way
home, he was startled to hear a cry
for help. Hurrying toward the sound,
he soon found himself by a fallen
tree that bridged a bubbling stream.
There, trapped in the water by the
tree's branches, was a leprechaun!
He must have been crossing the
stream and slipped. Now the water
slapped over the leprechaun's head,
and between gasping for air and
yelling for help he was nearly spent.
Donald O'Dell stepped out onto
a key branch and snatched the
leprechaun from the tree's grasp.

The poor wee man was shivering and wheezing. Donald O'Dell shrugged out of his sweater and wrapped the leprechaun in its warm woolen folds. Then, tucking him under an arm, he hurried home.

It was only a moment's work to kindle a fire and put the kettle on. Soon the leprechaun was sitting before the blaze, with his fingers curled around a steaming cup.

"It's a kind-hearted man you are entirely, Donald O'Dell," the leprechaun declared. "And you'll find me properly grateful. The saving of a leprechaun's life means a gift of leprechaun gold."

If he expected thanks, however, the leprechaun was sorely disappointed.

"I have enough for my needs," Donald replied. "You can keep the gold for yourself."

The leprechaun was dumbfounded. Never before had a man refused leprechaun gold. He pleaded with Donald O'Dell, cajoled him, debated the issue, and finally demanded that the man take the gold and be done with it. But Donald would not be swayed.

Finally the leprechaun prepared to leave. "But be assured," he told Donald O'Dell, "you'll accept the gold, one way or another."

The next morning Donald found
a pot of gold on the doorstep. He
shook his head, carried it to the
nearest fairie mound, and left it there.

That afternoon he reached for his coat, only to find the pockets weighed down with gold coins. He shrugged into the coat, walked to the fairie mound, and turned his pockets inside out.

So it went for the next week. Donald found gold everywhere he turned—in his shoes, pots, wagon, even his breakfast porridge. The path to the fairie mound soon grew well-worn.

Then the day arrived when Donald O'Dell went from dawn to dusk without seeing a single gold coin, barring that which he rightfully earned rethatching a roof.

"I expect the leprechaun has given up at last," he decided, feeling rather lonely.

The next morning, however, Donald had other things to worry him. When he went to milk his cow, Lettie, he found the latch to the byre undone and the cow gone entirely, even though he was sure he had latched the barn door securely the evening before.

There was nothing for it. He snatched a rope and took off, following the animal's tracks as they led through woods and meadows, hills and hollows. Indeed, he spent the whole day following after the beast.

Night swept in with the evening
rain and Donald could no longer
see the cow's tracks. It looked like he
would have to spend a damp night in
the dark woods. He sighed and was
about to settle under a tree when an
unexpected breeze whipped a branch
across his chest, turning him to one
side. From this new angle he spied a
light through the woods. Hurrying
toward it, he soon saw that it was a
window, lamplit and warm.

He pounded on the door.

When it was opened, his mouth dropped open as well.

Standing in the doorway was a beautiful woman. She smiled warmly and, glancing at the rope in his hands, said, "I don't suppose you might be the owner of that lovely cow that wandered into my barn just a few hours ago?"

Dumbly, Donald nodded.

The woman waved him inside. "It's cold you must be, and wet and worn out as well. Come away in and warm yourself by my fire. I'll feed you dinner, for your cow's already taken care of, and the two of you can spend the night in my barn."

Delighted, Donald accepted her invitation. Over dinner he discovered her name was Maureen, and she had lived there for several years tending her old grannie. Now Maureen was alone.

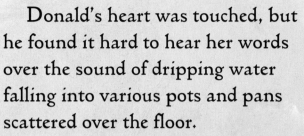

Donald's heart was touched, but he found it hard to hear her words over the sound of dripping water falling into various pots and pans scattered over the floor.

"It's the strangest thing," Maureen said. "The roof's been sound for years, with nary a problem, but this evening for some reason it began leaking horribly. I expect I'll have to find someone with the skill to rethatch it for me, but I don't know how I'll afford it."

"Ah," Donald O'Dell replied with a smile, "consider the job done, and paid in full as well for your hospitality, the fine meal, and the good company. I'll do the rethatching for you on the morrow, and gladly."

Maureen smiled and that was that. That night Donald O'Dell slept in the barn with Lettie, and he was up at the crack of dawn fixing Maureen's roof.

She hitched up her skirts and joined him. Oddly, the old thatch didn't look too bad. Still, by the time Donald O'Dell was finished, the only leak left was in his heart. He was taken entirely with Maureen.

They courted for a month or two, and then were wed. Donald O'Dell was happier than he'd ever been before.

"And not even leprechaun gold could have been better than this," he remarked to Maureen as they sat outside their cottage together.

She hurried as the night grew cold, and Donald went to check the barn.

"So, are you happy?" came a small voice.

"Aye, I am that," Donald replied upon discovering the leprechaun sitting on a railing in the byre. "But it's surprised I am to see you. I thought I'd offended your honor by my refusal of the gold. "

The leprechaun smiled. "And do you think cows wander free, and branches blow, and roofs leak without a wee bit of help? You've been paid in full, Donald O'Dell, for the saving of my life."

Donald looked puzzled. "I've taken no gold from you," he insisted.

"There's more than one kind of gold in this world," the leprechaun said, tipping his hat.

"It's away I'll be then," he continued. "Give my best to your bride, Maureen. She's a woman with hair of gold, and a heart to match."

And with a wink and a laugh, the leprechaun was gone.

To my brothers and sister and to their "leprechaun gold"
T.B.

To Liam Andrew
Best Wishes,
R.L.

Design by Lynn Braswell

Library of Congress Cataloging-in-Publication Data
Bateman, Teresa.
Leprechaun Gold / by Teresa Bateman;
illustrated by Rosanne Litzinger. −1st ed.
p.   cm.
Summary: When Donald O'Dell saves the life of
a leprechaun but refuses his offer of gold, he finds his good
deed rewarded in an unexpected fashion.
ISBN 0-8234-1344-6
[1. Leprechauns −Fiction.]   I. Litzinger, Rosanne, ill.   II. Title.
PZ7.B294435Lj   1998
[E]−dc21   97-19111   CIP   AC
ISBN 0-8234-1514-7 (pbk.)